Bath • New York • Cologne • Melbourne • Delhi
Hong Kong • Shenzhen • Singapore • Amsterdam

Today's Pirate Pledge:
Being a brave pirate means knowing
when to ask for help from your mateys.

One day, Jake and his crew are playing on the beach.
Suddenly, Skully notices something, "Package, ahoy!"
"Maybe it's treasure," says Cubby.
"Only one way to find out," says Jake. "Let's open 'er up!"

"Yo-ho, way to go!" says Jake. "It's a pogo stick!"
"What are we waiting for? Let's get jumping," says Izzy.

BOING, BOING! The crew takes turns jumping.
"Coconuts!" says Cubby, losing his balance. "This pogo stick is awfully springy!"

"Don't worry, Cubby," says Jake. "You just need to practise."
"I'll try again later," says Cubby.

"Smee, will you hold still?" says Captain Hook.
"Sorry, Cap'n, it's just that this wind is so . . . windy," says Smee.

"How am I ever going to get me hat down from that blasted tree?" Hook wonders aloud.
Just then, they hear . . . **BOING, BOING, BOING!**

"Did you see that?" asks Hook. "That puny pirate is using that *sproingy* thing to get a banana out of a tree!"

"That's nice, but I'm not ready for a snack," says Smee.

"No, you scurvy sea dog! If I had that bouncy thing, I could get me hat!" says Hook.

"Whoa!" says Cubby.
"Steady as she goes," says Jake. "You're doing great!"

YOINK! Hook uses his plunger hook to grab the pogo stick!

"Yay-hey, no way!" calls Izzy.

"That sneaky snook took our pogo stick," says Cubby.

BOING! "Look, Smee!" calls Hook. "I got me hat!"

"That's good, sir," calls Smee. "Now you had better stop before you hurt yourself."

"Nonsense," says Hook. "How could I possibly – ouch!"

"Smee! This blasted thing is broken," shouts Hook.
"Cap'n, where are you going?" shouts Smee.
"To get me hat!" calls Hook.

"Where could Captain Hook be?" Cubby wonders aloud.

Just then the crew hears . . . **BOING, BOING, BOING!**

"I hear Hook, but I don't see him anywhere," says Izzy.
"Look!" says Jake. "Pogo-stick tracks. If we follow them, I bet we'll find Captain Hook!"
"And our pogo stick," says Skully.

BOING, BOING!

"Aiieeee!" cries Captain Hook.
"Cap'n? Cap'n, where'd you go?" says Smee.
"Up here!" shouts Hook.

"I'll throw down the sproingy, boingy thing and you jump up here and get me," says Hook.

BOING! Smee bounces up, but he can't reach!

"Smee," shouts Captain Hook, "can't you do anything right?"

"There's Mr Smee," says Izzy.

"And our pogo stick!" says Skully.

"Thank goodness you sea pups are here," says Smee. "Here's your pogo stick. Sorry for all the trouble."

"That's okay, Mr Smee," says Jake. "Thanks for returning our pogo stick."

"Um, there's just one little problem," says Smee. "I'm afraid the Cap'n is, well ... up a tree."

"Crackers!" says Skully. "A pirate in a tree? Now I've seen everything!"

"Can you help him get down?" asks Smee.
"I don't need their help!" cries Hook.
"I can get down on my . . . whoooaaaaaaaa!"

"I know what will help Captain Hook get out of that tree," says Izzy. "Pixie Dust!"

"Come on, Mr Smee," says Jake.

Izzy sprinkles everyone with Pixie Dust!

"Oh my, I can fly!" says Smee.

"I don't need help," says Hook. "I'm fi– *ahhh!*"
Izzy sprinkles Hook with Pixie Dust just in time!
"Did I crash?" asks Hook.
"No, sir," says Smee. "Look!"

"I'm flying!" says Hook.
"Time to fly back to Pirate Island!" says Jake.
"Thanks for your help, sea pups," says Smee. "Now let's find your hat, Cap'n."

"Woo-hoo! Look at me! I'm a pogo master!" calls Cubby.
"I knew you'd get the hang of it if you tried!" says Jake. "You know, if Hook had just asked for help in the first place, he wouldn't have got into all that trouble."
"And we wouldn't have lost our pogo stick," says Skully.

"For solving pirate problems today, we earned eight Gold Doubloons!" says Jake. "Way to go, mateys!"

"I did it!" calls Cubby. "Whee!"

BOING, BOING, BOING!